GEORGE THE BRAVE

This book belongs to:

_____

_____

_____

George the Brave
Published in Great Britain in 2022 by Graffeg Limited.

First published by Mladá Fronta, Czech Republic, 2019.

Written by Eva Papoušková © 2019.
Illustrated by Galina Miklínová © 2019.

Designed and produced by Graffeg Limited © 2022.

Translation into English by Alexandra Büchler.

Graffeg Limited, 24 Stradey Park Business Centre,
Mwrwg Road, Llangennech, Llanelli, Carmarthenshire,
SA14 8YP, Wales, UK. Tel: 01554 824000.
www.graffeg.com.

The publisher acknowledges the financial support of the
Books Council of Wales. www.gwales.com.

ISBN 9781802580884

1 2 3 4 5 6 7 8 9

Eva Papoušková & Galina Miklínová

George The Brave

GRAFFEG

What's a wombat?

The common wombat (*Vombatus ursinus*) is a
hairy, slightly squat, chubby little animal with
short legs. It is quite cute and very rare. Wombats
live in Australia and are protected by law.
They are also protected by their very strong
bottoms, which they use to defend themselves by
thrusting them at their enemies. That's certainly
one of nature's more creative ways of standing
up for yourself!

George the Wombat has lots of friends.

One day, Fred the Kangaroo, Annie the Goose and little Lizzie the Mouse asked George if he wanted to come and play.

Mummy Wombat said he could.

'But be careful,' said Daddy Wombat.
'When you leave the burrow, remember to look
out for dangers. There are some animals that
would like to gobble us up.'

'How will I know which ones?' asked George.

'That's something that every wombat has to learn for themselves,' said Daddy Wombat. 'Then they'll know how to save their own skin.'

And he did a few moves, just to show that he knew.

George set out for the dark woods. He wasn't afraid, not really. He knew his skin was thick and covered with coarse hair, so saving it sounded pretty simple.

He soon caught up with Annie, Fred and Lizzie and they started to play hide and seek. It was George's turn to seek, so he shut his eyes and began to sing a little rhyme:

'One, two, three,
no fear for me!
Four, five, six,
I'm full of tricks.
Seven and eight
Not long to wait
Until nine and ten
When I'll find them all again.'

He opened his eyes...

...and there was Wilma the Fox.

'Well hello, little wombat!' she said with a sly smile.
'Welcome to my home in the dark wood.
Now, why don't you show me where you live?'

George froze.

'Why?' he asked.

'Because I'm Wilma the Fox and I say so,'
said the fox angrily.

George didn't like to be bossed around,
least of all by a fox.

But the truth was that Wilma had plans.

She liked the idea of gobbling up George,
but she also wanted to make a meal of the
whole wombat family.

George took a deep breath... he could smell danger.

He flexed his little legs and his hair bristled.
He had moves too, and one of them was...

...to RUN!!!

He ran and he ran, and as he ran he shouted back, 'No chance! You're not going to eat me.'

But Wilma chased after him, very fast! George ran in and out of the trees, this way and that, but the fox kept getting closer and closer until she could almost reach out for a tasty nibble...

...which was when George the Brave did the bravest thing of all. He stopped in his tracks and stuck out his big, strong, bony bottom!

It was too late for the fox to put on the brakes...

CRASHHHH!!!

All teeth and feet, Wilma collided with the little wombat's bottom. And as any wombat will tell you, that's where you'll find the hardest bone in their body. Ouch!

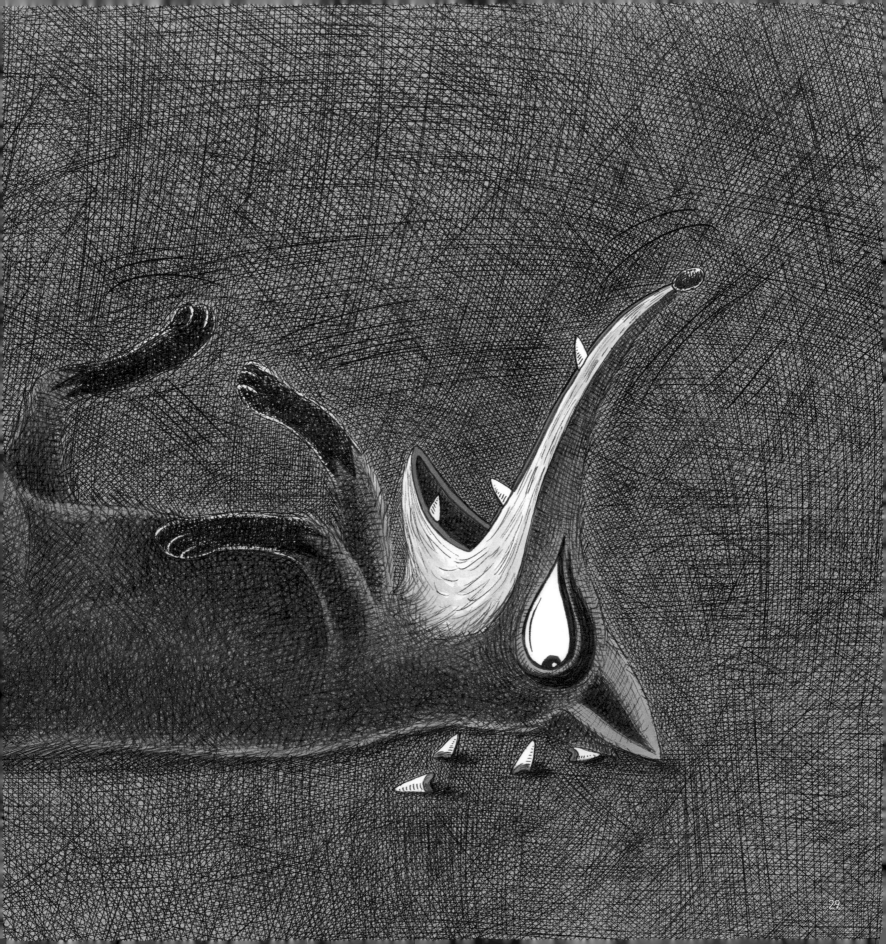

Crashing into George caused Wilma to lose
more than just her appetite...

...and when she finally got up, she crept
away quietly, her tail between her legs.

George went back to his friends.

'Why aren't you looking for us?' Lizzie wanted to know when he returned.

'What kept you so long?' asked Annie.

'Yes,' said Fred, 'I've been hiding in the bushes for ages and the twigs were tickling me!'

So George found all his friends without really having to look for them!

But the best thing of all? He learned that it's sometimes better to face your fears than to run away. Face them head on... well, sort of!

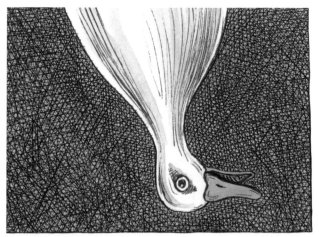

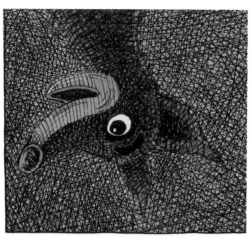